D0779649

Favori

Cowg and Cocoa
and
School Days

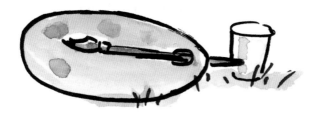

Favorite Stories from
from
Cowgirl Kate
and Cocoa
School Days

Written by **Erica Silverman**

Painted by **Betsy Lewin**

Green Light Readers
Houghton Mifflin Harcourt
Boston   New York

First Green Light Readers Edition, 2014

All rights reserved. Originally published as selections in *Cowgirl Kate and Cocoa:
School Days* in the United States by Harcourt Children's Books,
an imprint of Houghton Mifflin Harcourt Publishing Company, 2007.

Green Light Readers and its logo are trademarks of
Houghton Mifflin Harcourt Publishing Company,
registered in the United States of America and/or its jurisdictions.

For information about permission to reproduce selections from this book,
write to Permissions, Houghton Mifflin Harcourt Publishing Company,
215 Park Avenue South, New York, New York 10003.

www.hmhbooks.com

The text type was set in Filosofia Regular.
The illustrations in this book were done in watercolors
on Strathmore one-ply Bristol paper.

The Library of Congress cataloged the hardcover edition of
Cowgirl Kate and Cocoa: School Days as follows:
Silverman, Erica.
Cowgirl Kate and Cocoa: school days/Erica Silverman: illustrated by Betsy Lewin.
p. cm.
ISBN: 978-0-15-205378-9 hardcover
ISBN: 978-0-15-206130-2 paperback
Summary: Cocoa the horse does not want Cowgirl Kate to go to school without him.
[1.Cowgirls—Fiction. 2. Horses—Fiction. 3. First day of school—Fiction. 4. Schools—Fiction.]
I. Lewin, Betsy, ill. II. Title.
PZ7.S58625Cos 2007
[E]—dc22   2006011632

ISBN: 978-0-544-23017-0 GLR paper over board
ISBN: 978-0-544-23021-7 GLR paperback

Manufactured in China
SCP 10 9 8 7 6 5 4 3 2 1

4500461810

To Zoe and her big sister, Julia—with love —E.S.

To Claire Rose Reilly —B.L.

A New Friend

Cowgirl Kate got off the
school bus with a new friend.
"Cocoa," she said,
"I want you to meet Jenny."

Cocoa snorted.

Then he turned away.

"Cocoa, turn around," said Cowgirl Kate.

But Cocoa did not.

"Your horse does not like me," said Jenny.

"He just has to get to know you,"
said Cowgirl Kate.

Cowgirl Kate and Jenny played basketball.

"Cocoa, come play with us!"

called Cowgirl Kate.

But Cocoa did not.

Cowgirl Kate showed Jenny how to rope.

"Cocoa, come rope with us!"

called Cowgirl Kate.

But Cocoa did not.

Cowgirl Kate and Jenny had milk and cookies.

"Cocoa, come have a treat!"
called Cowgirl Kate.
Cocoa took a step closer,
but he did not join them.
"I hope he is not sick,"
said Cowgirl Kate.

Jenny's mother came to take Jenny home.

Jenny took a bag from her backpack.

"I forgot. I brought you a present," she said.

"Thank you," said Cowgirl Kate.

"See you in school."

Jenny and her mother drove away.

15

Cowgirl Kate hurried over to Cocoa.

"Cocoa," she asked, "are you sick?"

Cocoa sighed.

"I am heartsick," he said.

"You have school.

You have a new friend.

Soon you will forget all about me."

And he slouched away.

"Cocoa, wait!" she called.

"I have a yummy treat for you."

Cocoa stopped.

"Why would you give me a treat?" he asked.

"You don't like me anymore."

"Of course I like you," said Cowgirl Kate.

She stroked his neck.

"You are my best friend in the whole world."

"I am?" asked Cocoa.

"Yes, you are," said Cowgirl Kate.

"And nothing will ever change that."

"Not school?" he asked.

"Not school," she replied.

"Not a new friend?" he asked.

"Not a new friend," she replied.

Cocoa sighed.

Then he nudged her hand.

"I am ready for my treat now," he said.

Cowgirl Kate popped a peppermint candy
into his mouth.

"Yum!" he said.

"Where did you get such good treats?"

Cowgirl Kate smiled.

"They are a present from Jenny."

Cocoa grinned.

"I am happy we have a new friend," he said.

A Report

Cowgirl Kate was in her bedroom.

Cocoa stuck his head in the window.

"Play with me," he said.

"I can't," she replied.

"I'm writing a report."

"Can you play with a report?" he asked.

"No," she said.

"Then what good is it?" he asked.

"It has a good topic," she said.

"It's about horses."

"I know about horses," he said.

"I will help you."

So Cowgirl Kate took her
notebook outside.

"Read me your report," said Cocoa.

She read, "Horses have long, graceful tails."

"That's true," said Cocoa.

And he flicked his long,
graceful tail.

"Horses have long, flowing manes,"
she read.

"That's true, too," he said.

And he tossed his long, flowing mane.

"Horses come in black, white,

brown, tan, or gray," she read.

"Wait a minute," he said.

"I am the color of chocolate.

My mane and tail are the color of caramel."

"You are special," she said.

"That is very true," he agreed.

"What else should I write?"
asked Cowgirl Kate.
"I will show you," said Cocoa.
He trotted and cantered.

Horses like to trot and canter,
Cowgirl Kate wrote.

He galloped and jumped.
Horses like to gallop and jump,
she wrote.

He rolled on his back.

Horses like to roll on their backs, she wrote.

"And now," said Cocoa,

"can you guess what horses like to do

most of all?"

"Eat?" she guessed.

And she held out an apple.

Cocoa chomped it.

"Close," he said.

"But I was thinking of something else."

"Give me a hint," she said.

He gave her a nudge.

"Tag!" he squealed. "You're it!"

Cowgirl Kate laughed.

She wrote, *Most of all, horses*
like to play with their friends.

Then she put down her notebook
and chased Cocoa all
around the yard.

Erica Silverman is the author of a series of books about Cowgirl Kate and Cocoa, the original of which received a Theodor Seuss Geisel Honor. She has also written numerous picture books, including the Halloween favorite *Big Pumpkin*, as well as *Don't Fidget a Feather!*, *On the Morn of Mayfest*, and *Liberty's Voice*. Her new easy reader series, Lana's World, will be available from Green Light Readers soon. She lives in Los Angeles, California.

Betsy Lewin is the well-known illustrator of Doreen Cronin's *Duck for President*; *Giggle, Giggle, Quack*; and *Click, Clack, Moo: Cows That Type*, for which she received a Caldecott Honor. She lives in Brooklyn, New York.